Ducks
on the
Road

Ducks on the Road

A COUNTING ADVENTURE

ANITA LOBEL

A PAULA WISEMAN BOOK
SIMON & SCHUSTER BOOKS FOR YOUNG READERS
NEW YORK   LONDON   TORONTO   SYDNEY   NEW DELHI

SIMON & SCHUSTER BOOKS FOR YOUNG READERS
An imprint of Simon & Schuster Children's Publishing Division
1230 Avenue of the Americas, New York, New York 10020
© 2021 by Anita Lobel
For information about special discounts for bulk purchases,
please contact Simon & Schuster Special Sales at 1-866-506-1949 or business@simonandschuster.com.
The Simon & Schuster Speakers Bureau can bring authors to your live event.
For more information or to book an event, contact the Simon & Schuster Speakers Bureau
at 1-866-248-3049 or visit our website at www.simonspeakers.com.
Book design by Laurent Linn
The text for this book was set in Banda Regular.
The illustrations for this book were rendered in gouache and colored pencil with felt-tip pen touches.
Manufactured in China
1020 SCP
First Edition
2 4 6 8 10 9 7 5 3 1
Library of Congress Cataloging-in-Publication Data
Names: Lobel, Anita, author.
Title: Ducks on the road / Anita Lobel.
Description: First edition. | New York : Simon & Schuster Books for Young Readers, [2021] | "A Paula Wiseman Book." | Audience: Ages 4–8. |
Audience: Grades 2–3. | Summary: "Ten little ducks go for a walk with their parents but one by one,
they get distracted and go off on their own adventures, meeting new friends along the way"— Provided by publisher.
Identifiers: LCCN 2020029424 (print) | LCCN 2020029425 (ebook) |
ISBN 9781534465923 (hardback) | ISBN 9781534465930 (ebook)
Subjects: CYAC: Ducks—Fiction. | Animals—Fiction. | Counting.
Classification: LCC PZ7.L7794 Duc 2021 (print) | LCC PZ7.L7794 (ebook) |
DDC [E]—dc23
LC record available at https://lccn.loc.gov/2020029424
LC ebook record available at https://lccn.loc.gov/2020029425

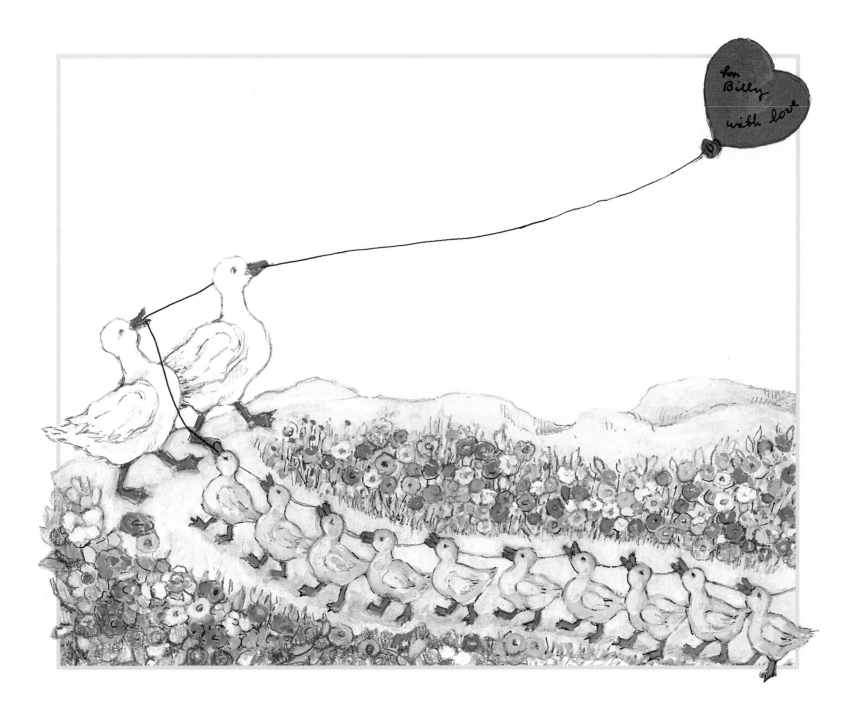

Ten little ducks walked on the road

behind Mama and Papa Duck.

Until the tenth little duck in line turned back to quack,

"Hello, Frog!"

Nine little ducks walked on the road

behind Mama and Papa Duck.

The ninth little duck in line

turned back to quack,

"Hello, Mouse!"

Eight little ducks walked on the road

behind Mama and Papa Duck.

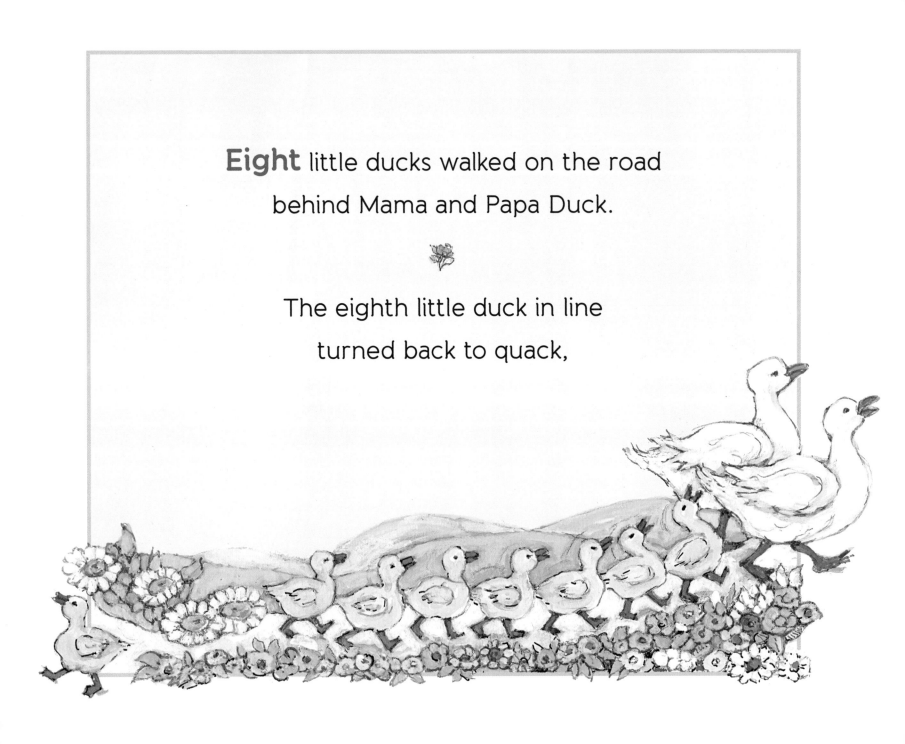

The eighth little duck in line

turned back to quack,

"Hello, Squirrel!"

Seven little ducks walked on the road
behind Mama and Papa Duck.

The seventh little duck in line
turned back to quack,

Six little ducks walked on the road

behind Mama and Papa Duck.

The sixth little duck in line

turned back to quack,

"Hello, Cat!"

Five little ducks walked on the road
behind Mama and Papa Duck.

The fifth little duck in line
turned back to quack,

"Hello, Dog!"

Four little ducks walked on the road

behind Mama and Papa Duck.

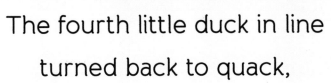

The fourth little duck in line

turned back to quack,

"Hello, Pig!"

Three little ducks walked on the road
behind Mama and Papa Duck.

The third little duck in line
turned back to quack,

"Hello, Sheep!"

Two little ducks walked on the road
behind Mama and Papa Duck.

The second little duck in line
turned back to quack,

"Hello, Owl!"

One little duck walked on the road

behind Mama and Papa Duck.

That first little duck in line

turned back to quack,

"Hello, Duck!"

Mama and Papa Duck turned around to see an empty road.

"Oh, no," they quacked. "Our little ducks are gone."

"No we are not," quacked eleven little ducks.

"Here we are!"

"One, two, three, four, five, six, seven, eight, nine, ten," counted Mama and Papa Duck!

"Eleven ducks!" Papa quacked.

"Even better," quacked Mama.